LONG TOM AND THE DEAD HAND

and other tales from
East Anglia and the Fen Country

LONG TOM AND THE DEAD HAND

and more tales from
East Anglia and the
Fen Country

KEVIN CROSSLEY-HOLLAND

Illustrated by

SHIRLEY FELTS

ANDRE DEUTSCH

*For Helen and George
and their grandchildren.*

Scholastic Children's Books
Scholastic Publication Ltd,
7–9 Pratt Street, London NW1 0AE

Scholastic Inc.,
730 Broadway, New York, NY 10003, USA

Scholastic Canada Ltd,
123 Newkirk Road, Richmond Hill,
Ontario L4C 3G5, Canada

Ashton Scholastic Pty Ltd,
P O Box 579, Gosford, New South Wales,
Australia

Ashton Scholastic Ltd,
Private Bag 1, Penrose, Auckland,
New Zealand

Text copyright © Kevin Crossley Holland 1992
Illustrations copyright © Shirley Felts 1992

ISBN 0 590 54014 9

Typeset by Contour Typesetters, Southall, London
Printed in Great Britain by The Bath Press, Avon

'I reckon it's best . . . to sort of believe nothing and everything, in a way.'

                                        –Old Lincolnshire man

'The Wildman' was first published by André Deutsch in 1976. Earlier versions of 'Samuel's Ghost' and 'Tom Tit Tot' first appeared in *British Folk Tales* (Orchard Books, 1987). 'Sea Tongue' was first published as part of the Listening and Reading series by the BBC in 1991.

I am most grateful to Jennifer Westwood and David Robinson for generously helping me with details of usage and translation in 'Cape of Rushes' and the Lincolnshire tales collected by Mrs. M.C. Balfour.

CONTENTS

Shonks and the Dragon

"Me?" said the Lord of the Manor of Pelham.

"You," said his daughter, namely Miss Eleanor. "You've no choice."

The Lord of the Manor, alias Sir Piers Shonks, crossed the huge trunk of his left leg over the huge trunk of his right leg, and sighed terribly. He stared into the fire until his eyeballs were burning.

"Mmm!" he said.

"Think of Sigurd and Beowulf and Carantoc!" exclaimed Eleanor.

"Tittle-tattle!" said Shonks.

"Assipattle, you mean," said Eleanor.

"Prattle-prattle," muttered her father.

"And now," exclaimed Eleanor, "Sir Piers Shonks!"

"Shonks, conks, honks," said the Lord of the Manor of Pelham. "Does it sound as if I'm a dragon-slayer?"

"Brave men need dragons," Eleanor said, and there were dragons dancing in her eyes.

"I don't need a dragon," said Shonks. "No, thank you."

"You do," said Eleanor. "To prove yourself. Anyhow, you've got no choice."

"I have!" said Shonks.

"You've no choice in the matter," Eleanor repeated. "You're the Lord of the Manor and he's the dragon of Brent Pelham. You've got to fight him."

The Lord of the Manor had a difficult dream. He had decided once and for all not to fight the dragon. "Dragons be

9

blowed!'' he could hear himself saying. "Dragons be blowed be blasted be Brummagemmed . . .''

But then the dragon of Brent Pelham came visiting. It shrithed into the manor and, most mysteriously, seemed to turn into his daughter, so that whenever Shonks looked at Eleanor, he seemed to be looking at the dragon.

And then, even more strangely, Shonks dreamed he was turning into the dragon himself. He was becoming a wrongdoer, an evil flame-thrower, and the very people who depended on him now began to avoid him.

So when Shonks woke up, sweating and cold, after a horrible argument with his sheets and blankets, he knew his daughter was right. He had no choice! In the name of every man, woman and child living in Brent Pelham – why! in his own name, modest as it was, he had to fight the dragon.

"Brute!'' said Shonks, most miserably. "Biggonet, bastion, blabber, bodily, bone-white . . .'' On and on he went, as if he were a walking lexicon. But quite what he was talking about is impossible to tell.

If anything, Sir Piers Shonks' armour was even more reluctant than its owner. It had long since gone into retirement; its shoulders and elbows and knees and ankles creaked and cracked, and for year after year armies of clothes-moths had picknicked in the woollen padding inside the helmet.

"Darn!'' grumbled Shonks. And then, "Drat! Devil's teeth!''

"Courage!'' said Eleanor, helping her father secure his sword-belt.

"That's what you're going to need, my girl,'' said Shonks.

"Me?'' said Eleanor.

"I'm taking you with me.''

Eleanor's eyes opened sky-wide.

"You're the best man I've got,'' said her father. "Anyhow,

I'm between squires."

So while the armourer oiled Shonks' groaning joints and the blacksmith stropped his sword and spear, Eleanor stepped upstairs and changed into the best dress in her garderobe.

"And now for my snood," she said. "Snood! I hate that word."

The dragon had made a mess of Brent Pelham. He had set fire to two of the embattled old oaks, guardians of the village green since the days of King Alfred. He had flattened whole hedgerows. And worst of all, he had knocked down seven little cruck-cottages, eaten three harvest-heavy pigs and dozens of chickens, and blown out the new nativity window at the east end of the church.

"Blessed Virgin preserve me!" said Shonks.

"She's nothing but glass splinters," Eleanor said. "All over the churchyard. What about the saints? Saint Martha? Saint George? Philip? And Pol?"

Father and daughter galloped along the ride between Great Pepsells and Little Pepsells, and Shonks' three best hounds galloped beside them – and all three were so fleet and light of foot that one old man, rather the worse for wear, was quite certain they had wings. In both fields, the poor corn looked as if it had run this way and run that way and pressed its ears to the ground . . .

And underground, in its lair beneath the roots of the great yew tree, the dragon heard them coming. It rose to the light.

"Dear God!" said Shonks. And then, "BACK! BACK!" he shouted at Eleanor. "My beautiful! Brightest! Best! And everything else beginning with B!"

Then Shonks dismounted and he and the dragon joined battle. Shonks raised his ashen spear and the dragon raised its head. It bellowed, it blew out vile sulphurous smoke.

Many is the battle won by mistake. When the dragon

threw fire at the man, the man stepped sideways to avoid the jet-stream; he stepped and tripped, fell forward, and falling thrust his spear right down the dragon's throat.

"Aargh!" said the dragon.

Gargle and spit! Humans, horses and hounds – and the birds in heaven itself – were coated with flecks of pink foam. It made the three hounds grin and sneeze.

"Listen to the birds!" shouted Shonks. "Life! That's what they're singing. Lifelife. Life!"

"Father," called Eleanor. Quickly she dismounted, then she picked up her skirts, ran towards Shonks over the bumpy ground, and threw herself into his metal embrace.

When Sir Piers and Miss Eleanor had disentangled themselves, they saw a man leaning quite nonchalantly against one side of the dead dragon.

"Good morning!" he said, and he smiled and blew on his long white fingers. He was very slight, and his hair and eyes were both dark. "Good morning to you both!"

"Where have you come from?" asked Shonks.

"Immediately," said the man, "from Cambridge. Or do you mean, how did I get here?" asked the man, smiling. "Is that what you mean?"

"Well," said Shonks, "I haven't seen you around here before."

"No," said the man, still smiling, and he flexed his fingers. "I live in your hereafter."

"My hereafter?"

"So we should be seeing plenty of one another before too long."

"What do you mean?" asked Eleanor, and she took her father's arm. "What's your name?"

"I have many names," said the little man quite affably. "Some say, the *great dragon*."

"I know my Book of Revelation," said Shonks quickly. "I know who you are."

"Then you know why I'm here," said the man.

"Saint Matthew and Saint Mark and Saint Luke and Saint John," murmured Shonks. "May they trample the dragon under their feet."

"I see you've killed my servant," said the little man. "Well! A life for a life! You've killed the dragon of Brent Pelham; so when you die, Piers Shonks, I'll have you."

"No!" cried Shonks. "Not! Never! Numquam!"

"Oh, yes, Shonks. I'll have you, body and soul."

"Not if I'm buried inside the church. I'll have them bury me inside the church."

"Inside the church, outside the church, it doesn't matter to me, I'll have you either way."

"Never!" shouted Shonks again.

The man winked at Miss Eleanor. "And you, my pretty," he said, "you're my witness."

Piers Shonks shook off one of his gauntlets and bowed his head and crossed himself. "I commend my soul to God," he said. "And when I die, my body will lie – lie and sleep – exactly where I choose."

The man arched his black eyebrows and smiled at Shonks. There were flames in his freezing eyes. Then he simply stamped one foot and disappeared.

Years passed and Sir Piers Shonks became old. He became very old and his mouth grew dry.

"Dreary, devil, dragon, dropsical, Dunstable," muttered Shonks as he lay on his death-bed. "And everything else beginning with D." And then, rallying himself considerably, "Carry me outside! Bring me my longbow!"

Six manor servants lifted the Lord of the Manor of Pelham, still lying on his bed. They carried him down to the moat, and there Miss Eleanor put his longbow in his speckled hands.

"Cut from the great yew – the one between Great Pepsells and Little Pepsells," said Eleanor. "Do you remember, father?"

"Oh, do shut up!" said Shonks. "Give me an arrow!"

Shonks screwed up his eyes and drew in his lips and notched an arrow.

"Now listen to me!" he said. "I'll shoot this one arrow and then I'll die."

The manor servants began to get down on their knees in the wet grass.

"Bury me wherever this arrow falls. Wherever it falls. Do you understand me?"

The six servants nodded.

"As you choose, father," said Miss Eleanor.

"Inside or outside, indeed!" grumbled Shonks. "Inside or outside. I'll show him."

Then the Lord of the Manor of Pelham summoned up all the remaining strength in his body. He drew back the bowstring as far as he could, and then even a little further, and released it.

The bowstring hummed and shuddered and fell still, but the arrow flew singing through the bright air. It rose and sped and dipped, dipped and stuck into the north wall of Brent Pelham church.

So Shonks died smiling. Not inside the church, not outside the church: he was buried deep within the church wall. The devil reached out his long white fingers and he still could not touch him.

Long Tom and the Dead Hand

.....◆.....

Long Tom Pattison was a wild slip of a lad. He was always larking around. No one had a word to say against him, though: for all his tricks, he was a decent lad – just too full of fun, and too waggle-headed to stop and think things through, most of the time.

There were heaps of stories about the marsh surrounding the village where Tom lived, stories about boggarts and horrors and the like. People were scared of gruesome things and never went out at night on their own.

After an evening in the inn, the men all hung around, and all walked home together. And even then, they disliked the shadows and the dark corners, and fingered their safe-keeps all the way home. Almost everyone had a sort of charm to keep the evil things away – bits of paper with verses out of the Bible, crinkled up in a nutshell; three straws and a four-leafed clover tied with the hair of a dead man; spells written by a wise woman; or maybe the clippings of a dead woman's nails. If you could get them, they were the best safe-keep of all.

Well, Long Tom was just about the only lad in the place without a safe-keep, and everyone said that one day he'd regret it. His mother was always begging and beseeching him to carry the charm she'd got from old Molly, the wise woman who lived next to the mill.

But Tom only laughed and refused to take it. At closing-time in the inn, he mocked the men because they were afraid of the dark; and he pretended to see things in the black corners, to make them more scared than ever.

But one night the men rounded on Tom. "That's all right

your making fun of us,'' they said. ''But if you met a bogle, or had to cross the marsh in the dark, you'd be no better than the rest of us.''

Maybe Tom had drunk more beer than he ought to have done. Anyhow the silly lad got all fired up. ''I'm afraid of nothing,'' he shouted, ''nothing you can see and nothing you can't see. I'll cross the marsh alone, by lantern-light, on the darkest night of the year.''

There was a noisy argument in the inn that evening, but at last they calmed down a bit, and it was agreed that Long Tom would walk the path across the marsh, and round by the willow-snag, on the very next night. ''And if you decide against it,'' said the men, ''you must stop getting at other people for being afraid of the dark.''

''By God!'' said the stupid creature. ''I won't break my word, I can promise you that. What a pack of fools you are! Why should I come to harm in the marsh, when I have to cross it almost every day as part of my job?''

Long Tom sounded so bold and confident that some of the younger lads began to think maybe he was right after all, and the bogles weren't as black – as the saying goes – as they were painted. But the older men knew better than that. They shook their heads and hoped no harm would come of the lad's disbelieving ways.

Well, they all thought Tom would regret his words next day, when he'd thought about things a bit; but for all that, as soon as it got dark the men and lads met at the corner of the green lane, near the cottage where Tom lived with his mother.

When they got there, they could hear the old woman in the kitchen, sobbing and scolding Tom; and they began to wonder whether, after all, the lad really meant to cross the marsh alone. And after a while the door was flung open, and out came Tom laughing like mad, and pulling away from his old mother, who was trying to put something into his pocket, and sobbing fit to break her heart.

"No, mother," Tom was saying, "I tell you, I'll have none of your charms and bobberies. Stop snivelling, will you? I'll be back before long, safe and sound. Don't you be a fool like the rest of them, do you hear me?"

Then Long Tom snatched the lantern from the old woman, and, mocking and laughing at the lads, he ran off toward the marsh. At this, some of the men tried to stop Tom, and begged him not to go.

"If you won't take back your words," said one man – it was Willie Kirby – "I'll take back mine. You can mock us as much as you like, but stay here! Don't go down to the marsh! You don't know what might happen to you."

But Tom only laughed and snapped his fingers in Willie's face. "That for the boggart!" he cried. "And for you too!" And away he ran.

Then the old men waggled their heads, and they went home hoping for the best, but feeling terribly uneasy. Some of the youngsters, though, were ashamed to look afraid, seeing as Tom gave nothing for the horrors, and maybe a dozen of them followed him down the paths that led to the marsh. They weren't all that sure of themselves, and were scared enough when they felt the earth was squishy underfoot, and saw the glint of the lantern falling on the black water holes next to the path. But on they went – Tom perhaps thirty steps ahead, singing and whistling as bold as can be, and the lads behind, bunched close together but getting less afraid as they went further and further into the marsh without seeing anything of the bogles and horrors.

As they drew near the willow-snag, though, the wind came up the valley with a long, soughing moan – chill and damp it came straight from the sea – wailing as if it carried inside it all the evil things that live in the darkness and the shadows. Out went Tom's lantern, and the soughing wind was so chill and scary that the lad stopped singing, and stood stock-still by the willow-snag.

19

The boys behind felt worse than Tom did: they dared not go back and they didn't dare go forward, they could only stand trembling and praying and squeezing their safe-keeps in the darkness, waiting for something to happen.

And then, the things that Tom had disbelieved in, they came, they did – the horrors of the air, and the horrors of the waters, and the slimy, creeping things, and the crying, wailing things – until the night, that had been so quiet and still, was full of moving shadows and dim grinning faces with blazing eyes and wailing voices.

Closer and closer they came round Long Tom as he stood with his back against the snag and his hands in his pockets, trying to keep his spirits up. The very darkness seemed alive with shapes, and the air was thick with their wailing.

The lads behind Tom were down on their knee-bones by now, praying for dear life, and calling on the saints, and the Virgin Mary, and the wise women, to save them. They could see Tom was standing with his back against the stump, and saw his white face and furious eyes through the shadows thronging between them.

And after a while, so they said afterwards, they heard Tom shouting and swearing as the black things came closer and closer; they were only able to catch glimpses of him, and then Tom threw up his arms, and he appeared to be fighting and struggling with the things around him; and by-and-by they could hear nothing but the skirling and laughing and wailing and moaning of the horrors, and see nothing but the shifting blackness of the crowding shapes, until all at once the darkness opened out and right in front of them they saw Long Tom standing by the snag, with his face white as death and with staring eyes. He was holding on to the willow with one hand, and the other was stretched out and gripped by a Hand without a body, that pulled him and pulled him with terrible strength towards the black bog next to the path.

The lads could see the light that flickered across Tom's

face came from the Dead Hand itself, with its rotting flesh dropping off the mouldy bones, and its dreadful fingers tightly gripping Tom's hand, as if the two hands had grown together. More and more strongly the Hand pulled, and at last Tom let go of the willow-snag, and was dragged away and off the path and, with a great shriek, maybe like a soul in hell, he was swallowed up in the darkness.

After this, the lads could scarcely say what had happened to them. The horrors came round them, and skirled and mocked them; they never harmed the lads because of their safe-keeps and their prayers, but they howled at them, and plucked at their clothing, until the poor things were mad with terror and sick with the awfulness of it.

One lad crept up the path on his hands and knee-bones and that's how he got out of the terrible bog; another was found lying next in a water-hole; and so, one by one, the villagers who came into the marsh got them all out. But the lads were out of their wits with fear, and they couldn't bring themselves to tell what had happened to Long Tom. Each time someone asked where he might be, they began to screech and sob with terror, so the villagers could get nothing out of the poor creatures that night.

The next day, though, the villagers heard all about Tom, and of course they went into the marsh in the good sunlight, and looked and looked for him. His poor mother called and cried out for him; she swore she couldn't live without her only son, her baby, and she a poor widow woman.

But the villagers couldn't find a trace of the lad. Then the women took the old mother back to her cottage, and tried to comfort her and hush her sobbing; but the poor creature tore away from them like a mad thing, and ran back to the marsh, and began calling and calling on her son, just as before, to come back to his poor lonely mother, and she a widow.

Over and over again the old woman cried out and wailed for her son, and the villagers could do nothing to hush her.

So they had to leave her be, for they could find not a trace of Long Tom.

As the days passed by, people went back to work; the boys who had followed Tom into the marsh began to creep about, scared and white and trembling; you might have thought things were much the same as they had been before. But Tom didn't come back. And night after night the lamp flared in the window of the cottage at the end of the lane, and the old woman sat up waiting for her boy, and the door stood open from sundown until dawn. And all day long, the old woman wandered along the marsh paths, calling and calling on her son to come back, come back to his mother, and she a widow!

The village people were kind of afraid of the old woman, and kept out of her way when she came past. She was so grey and bent and wrinkled and sorrowful, and flitted about like one of the bog things themselves.

So the days wore on, and it was the seventh evening since Tom had been dragged into the marsh. Some of the villagers were sauntering along the edge of the marsh, as they had taken to doing since the lad had been lost, when all at once, just before dark, they heard a great cry – and a second great cry, so full of wonder and joy that it was sort of gruesome to hear it. And as they stood there, waiting and wondering, they saw the old mother scurrying towards them along one of the marsh-paths, beckoning and waving like mad.

It was a bit scary, but nonetheless the villagers followed her out into the marsh, as fast as their bones would carry them. They caught up with her at the willow-snag – and there sat Long Tom with his back against the stump, and his feet in the water! There he sat, with his mother sobbing over him, and kissing every inch of him. But my faith! What a changed creature he was! His back was bent, his limbs were shaking like an old grandfather, his great blazing eyes glared out of his white wrinkled face, and his hair, once so brown and curly, was white and grey and hanging down in long straggling wisps.

With one hand, Tom kept pointing, pointing at something, and staring at something, as if he could see nothing else; and where the other hand ought to have been, the hand gripped by the dreadful Dead Fingers, there was nothing but a ragged, bleeding stump – Tom's hand had been pulled clean off!

There he sat, gibbering and grinning, grinning at the horrors, which nobody but himself could see! Ah! And no one ever did know just what he could see, and what he had seen during those awful nights and days which he spent with the horrors; no one ever knew where he had been, or how he had come back, except what that bleeding stump could tell them of a terrible struggle with the awful Hand, a tugging for dear life. For after they found him by the snag, with his mother crooning over him and fondling him, Long Tom Pattison never spoke another word.

All day long he would sit in the sun, or sit by the fire, grinning and grinning; and all night long he wandered along the edge of the marsh, screeching and moaning like a thing in torment, with his poor old mother tagging along like a dog at heel, begging and praying him to come home. And when one of Tom's old friends stopped by to have a look at him, Tom's mother would pat the silly poor creature's head and say: "He said he'd come home, and he did; my baby did come to his mother, and she a widow woman."

That's all there is to it. It's not much of a story – but as you can see, it was all a result of Tom's disbelieving ways. The poor creature didn't live for more than a year. And when he died, the village women took his mother away from his corpse, and tried their best to stop her from going back to him; but when they came to put the lad into his coffin for the funeral, there she was, propped up in one corner of the bed, with Tom in her arms. She was nursing him as she used to do when he was a little thing, and she was dead – dead – like her son lying across her knees.

People said the old woman was smiling like a sleeping baby; but on Tom's face – ah! there was an awful look, as if the horrors had followed him and fought to have him for themselves.

Long Tom couldn't rest in his grave in the churchyard, and on dark nights before the marsh was drained, he went moaning up and down along the edge of the bog, with his old mother trailing after him. And through the shrieking and sobbing, people said they could hear the old woman's voice, whimpering and calling out, as she'd done so often in life: "He came back to his mother, he did, and she a widow woman."

Tom Tit Tot

There was once a little old village where a woman lived with her giddy daughter. The daughter was just sixteen, and sweet as honeysuckle.

One fine morning, the woman made five meat pies and put them in the oven. But then a neighbour called round and they were soon so busy gossiping that the woman forgot about the pies. By the time she took them out of the oven, their crusts were as hard as the bark of her old oak tree.

"Daughter," she says, "you put them there pies in the larder."

"My! I'm that hungry," says the girl.

"Leave them there and they'll come again," says the woman. She meant, you know, that the crusts would get soft.

"Well!" the girl says to herself, "if they'll come again, I'll eat them now." And so she set to work and ate them all, first and last.

When it was supper time, the woman felt very hungry.

"I could just do with one of them there pies," she says. "Go and get one off the shelf. They'll have come again now."

The girl went and looked, and there was nothing on the shelf but an empty dish. "No!" she calls. "They haven't."

"Not none of them?" says the woman.

"No!" calls the girl. "No! Not none."

"Well!" says the woman. "Come again or not, I'll have one for my supper."

"You can't if they haven't come," says the girl.

"I can though," says the woman. "Go and get the best one."

"Best or worst," says the girl, "I've eaten the lot, so you can't have one until it's come again."

The woman was furious. "Eaten the lot! You dardle-dumdue!"

The woman carried her spinning wheel over to the door and to calm herself, she began to spin. As she spun she sang:

"My daughter's ate five; five pies today.
My daughter's ate five; five pies today."

The King came walking down the street and heard the woman.

"What were those words, woman?" he says. "What were you singing?"

The woman felt ashamed of her daughter's greed. "Well!" she says, beginning to spin again:

"My daughter's spun five; five skeins today.
My daughter's spun five; five skeins today."

"Stars of mine!" exclaims the king. "I've never heard of anyone who could do that." The king raised his eyebrows and looked at the girl, so sweet and giddy and sixteen; he stared at a flowerbed and rubbed his nose.

"Five today," says the woman.

"Look here!" says the king. "I want a wife and I'll marry your daughter. For eleven months of the year," he says, "she can eat as much food as she likes, and buy all the dresses she wants; she can keep whatever company she wishes. But during the last month of the year, she'll have to spin five skeins every day; and if she doesn't, I'll cut off her head."

"All right!" says the woman. "That's all right, isn't it, daughter?"

The woman was delighted at the thought that her daughter was going to marry the king himself. She wasn't worried about the five skeins. "When that comes to it," she said to her daughter later, "we'll find a way out of it. More likely, though, he'll have clean forgotten about it."

So the king and the girl were married. And for eleven months the girl ate as much food as she liked and bought all the dresses she wanted and kept whatever company she wished.

As the days of the eleventh month passed, the girl began to think about those skeins and to wonder whether the king was thinking about them too. But the King said not a word, and the girl was quite sure he had forgotten them.

On the very last day of the month, though, the king led her up to a room in the palace she had never set eyes on before. There was nothing in it but a spinning wheel and a stool.

"Now, my dear," says the king, "you'll be shut in re tomorrow with some food and some flax. And if you haven't spun five skeins before dark, your head will be cut off."

Then away went the king to do everything a king has to do.

Well, the girl was that frightened. She had always been such a giddy girl, and she didn't know how to spin. She didn't know what to do next morning, with no one beside her and no one to help her. She sat down on a stool in the palace kitchen and heavens! how she did cry.

All of a sudden, however, she heard a sort of knocking low down on the door. So she stood up and opened it, and what did she see but a small little black thing with a long tail. That looked up at her, all curious, and that said, "What are you crying for?"

"What's that to you?" says the girl.

"Never you mind," that says. "You tell me what you're crying for."

"That won't do me no good if I do," the girl replies.

"You don't know that," that said, and twirled its tail round.

"Well!" she says. "That won't do me no harm if that don't do me no good." So she told him about the pies and the skeins and everything.

"This is what I'll do," says the little black thing. "I'll come to your window every morning and take the flax; and I'll bring it back all spun before dark."

"What will that cost?" she asks.

The thing looked out of the corners of its eyes and said. "Every night I'll give you three guesses at my name. And if you haven't guessed it before the month's up, you shall be mine."

The girl thought she was bound to guess its name before the month was out. "All right," she says. "I agree to that."

"All right!" that says, and lork! how that twirled that's tail.

Well, next morning, the king led the girl up to the room, and the flax and the day's food were all ready for her.

"Now there's the flax," he says. "And if it isn't spun before dark, off goes your head!" Then he went out and locked the door.

The king had scarcely gone out when there was a knocking at the window.

The girl stood up and opened it and sure enough, there was the little old thing sitting on the window ledge.

"Where's the flax?" it says.

"Here you are!" she says. And she gave it the flax.

When it was early evening, there was a knocking again at the window. The girl stood up and opened it, and there was the little old thing, with five skeins over its arm.

"Here you are!" that says, and it gave the flax to her. "And now," it says, "what's my name?"

"What, is that Bill?" she says.

"No!" it says, "that ain't." And that twirled that's tail.

"Is that Ned?" she says.

"No!" it says, "that isn't." And that twirled that's tail.

"Well, is that Mark?" says she.

"No!" it says, "that ain't." And that twirled that's tail faster, and away it flew.

When the girl's husband came in, the five skeins were ready for him. "I see I shan't have to kill you tonight, my dear," he says. "You'll have your food and your flax in the morning," he says, and away he went to do everything a king has to do.

Well, the flax and the food were made ready for the girl each day, and each day the little black impet used to come in the morning and return in the early evening. And each day and all day the girl sat thinking of names to try out on the impet when it came back in the evening. But she never hit on the right one! As time went on towards the end of the month, the impet looked wickeder and wickeder, and that twirled that's tail faster and faster each time she made a guess.

So they came to the last day of the month but one. The impet returned in the early evening with the five skeins, and it said. "What, hain't you guessed my name yet?"

"Is that Nicodemus?" she says.

"No! 't'ain't," that says.

"Is that Samuel?" she says.

"No! 't'ain't," that says.

"Ah! well. Is that Methusalem?" says she.

"No! 't'ain't that either," it says. And then that looks at the girl with eyes like burning coals.

"Woman," that says, "there's only tomorrow evening, and then you'll be mine!" And away it flew!

Well, the girl felt terrible. Soon, though, she heard the king coming along the passage; and when he had walked into the room and seen the five skeins, he says, "Well, my dear! So far as I can see, you'll have your skeins ready tomorrow evening too. I reckon I won't have to kill you, so I'll have my supper in here tonight." Then the king's servants brought up his supper, and another stool for him, and the two of them sat down together.

The king had scarcely eaten a mouthful before he pushed back his stool, and waved his knife and fork, and began to laugh.

"What is it?" asks the girl.

"I'll tell you," says the king. "I was out hunting today, and I got lost and came to a clearing in the forest I'd never seen before. There was an old chalkpit there. And I heard a kind of sort of humming. So I got off my horse and crept up to the edge of the pit and looked down. And do you know what I saw? The funniest little black thing you ever set eyes on! And what did that have but a little spinning wheel! That was spinning and spinning, wonderfully fast, spinning and twirling that's tail. And as it spun, it sang,

> "Nimmy nimmy not,
> My name's Tom Tit Tot."

Well, when the girl heard this, she felt as if she could have jumped out of her skin for joy; but she didn't say a word.

Next morning, the small little black thing looked wicked as wicked when it came for the flax. And just before it grew dark, she heard it knocking again at the window pane. She opened the window and that came right in on to the sill. It was grinning from ear to ear, and ooh! that's tail was twirling round so fast.

"What's my name?" that says, as it gave her the skeins.

"Is that Solomon?" she says, pretending to be afraid.

"No! 't'ain't," that says, and it came further into the room.

"Well, is that Zebedee?" she says again.

"No! 't'ain't," says the impet. And then that laughed and twirled that's tail until you could scarcely see it.

"Take time, woman," that says. "Next guess, and you're

mine." And that stretched out its black hands towards her.

The girl backed away a step or two. She looked at it, and then she laughed and pointed a finger at it and sang out:

> "Nimmy nimmy not,
> Your name's Tom Tit Tot."

Well, when the impet heard her, that gave an awful shriek and away it flew into the dark. She never saw it again.

The Gipsy Woman

(a sequel to 'Tom Tit Tot')

···•———◆◉▶———•···

Well, the girl ate well and dressed well and enjoyed the best of company for the whole of the next year, until the eleventh month was almost over.

And then her husband says to her: "Well, my dear, today's the end of the month. Tomorrow you'll have to begin again, and spin your five skeins every day."

The girl thought her husband had clean forgotten about the skeins, and now she didn't know what to do. She knew she couldn't count on Tom Tit Tot any longer, and she couldn't spin a mite herself: and so her head would have to come off!

Poor Toad, she sat herself down on a stool in the bakehouse, and she cried as if her heart would break.

All at once, the girl heard someone knocking at the door. So she got up and unlocked it, and there stood a gipsy woman, as brown as a berry.

"Well, well! What's all this to-do?" she says. "What are you crying like that for?"

"Get away, you gipsy woman," says she. "Don't you poke your nose in where you're no use."

"Tell me what's wrong, and maybe I *shall* be some use," says the woman. And she looked so understanding that the girl stood up and told her.

"Is that all?" she says. "I've helped people out of worse holes than this, and now I'll help you."

"Ah! But what will you ask for helping me?" says the girl, for she was thinking of how she'd almost given herself away to the bad-tempered little black impet.

35

"I don't want anything except the best suit of clothes you have got," says the gipsy.

"You shall have them, and welcome," says the girl, and she ran and opened the chest where her best dresses and things were, and gave one to the woman, and a brooch of gay gold. For she thought to herself, "If she's a cheat and can't help me, and my head is cut off, it won't matter if I *have* given away my best gown."

The woman looked delighted when she saw the gown. "Now then," she says, "you'll have to ask all the people you know to a damned fine party, and I'll come to it."

Well, the girl went to her husband, and she says: "My dear, seeing as this is the last night before I spin, I should like to have a party."

"All right, my dear," he says.

So the people were all asked, and they came in their best clothes; silks and satins, and all manner of fine things.

Well, they all had a grand supper with the best of foods, and they enjoyed themselves a great deal. But the gipsy woman never came near them, and the girl's heart was in her mouth.

One of the lords, who was tired of dancing, said it wasn't long off bull's noon, and it was time to go.

"No, no! Stay a little longer," the girl says. "Let's have a game of blind man's bluff first." So they began to play.

Just then the door flew open, and in came the gipsy woman. She'd washed herself, and combed her hair, and wound a gay handkerchief round her head, and put on the grand gown, so that she looked like a Queen.

"Stars of mine!" says the king. "Who's that?"

"Oh! That's a friend of mine," says the girl. And she watched to see what the gipsy would do.

"What, are you playing blind man's bluff?" says the gipsy. 'I'll join in with you."

And so she did. But what was in her pocket but a little pot

36

of cold cart-grease? And as she ran around, she dipped her hand in this grease, and smudged it on people as she brushed past them.

That wasn't long before someone cried out. "Oh lord! There's some nasty stuff on my gown."

"Why, it's on my dress too," says another. "That must have come off you."

"No! That it didn't. You've put it on me." And then almost everyone began to shout and quarrel with each other, each one thinking someone else had gone and smirched them.

Then the king stepped forward and listened to the hullaballoo. The ladies were crying, and the gentlemen were shouting, and all their fine clothes were daubed with grease.

"Why, what's this?" he says, for there was a great mark on the sleeve of his coat. He smelt it and turned up his nose. "That's cart-grease," he says.

"No, it isn't," says the gipsy woman. "That comes off my hand. That's spindle grease."

"Why, what's spindle grease?" he says.

"Well," she says, "I've been a great spinner in my time, and I spun and spun and spun five skeins a day. And because I spun so much, the spindle grease worked into my hands; and now, as often as I wash them, I dirty every thing I touch. And if your wife spins as much as I do, she'll have spindle grease like I have."

The king looked at his coat sleeve, and he rubbed it and sniffed at it and then he said to his wife: "Look here, my dear, and listen to what I say. If ever I see you again with a spindle in your hands, your head will go off."

So the girl never had to spin again.

And that's all.

That's None of Your Business

·····•————◆————•·····

That clock! It was like a piece of icing done by a goddess, dropped out of heaven.

It was white as white, and inlaid with little mirrors and misty pearls. The tick-and-tock of it were as close and comforting as the beats of your own heart, and the music it made on the hour, every hour, seemed to come straight from paradise.

Every boy and girl in the village came round to listen to it, and look at it. How longingly they looked at it!

So when they grew up and I grew old, and had little time for grand possessions, I thought I just might give it away. I said I'd give it to whoever could mind his own business – or her own business, for that matter – for a whole year.

At the end of the year, a year all but a few minutes, there was a knock on the door. A young man had come to ask for the clock.

"I've minded my own business for a whole year," he said.

I believed him. He was a dull sort of lad, the kind that never asks questions and doesn't seem too interested in other people or the wonders of the world.

As I went into the next room to fetch the clock, I called out, "You're the second young man, you know, who's come to claim the clock."

"The second!" exclaimed the young man. "Why didn't the first one get it?"

"That's none of your business," I said. "And *you* won't get the clock."

So I left the clock on the mantelpiece. There it is! Inlaid

with little mirrors and misty pearls. It's like a piece of icing done by a goddess, dropped out of heaven.

A Pitcher of Brains

Near here and not so long ago either, there lived a fool. And he was such a fool that he was always getting into trouble, and being laughed at by everyone. So he decided to buy a pitcher of brains.

"You can get everything you want from the wise woman who lives on the hilltop," people told him. "She deals in potions and herbs and spells and things, and can tell you everything that will happen to you or your family.

So the fool went to his mother and asked her whether he should go to the wise woman and buy a pitcher of brains.

"That you should," she said. "You need them badly enough. And if I were to die, my son, who would take care of a poor fool like you? You're no more fit to look after yourself than a newborn baby." The fool's mother wagged her forefinger. "Mind your manners, and speak to her nicely, my lad. The wise people are easily put out."

So off went the fool after his tea, and there was the wise woman, sitting by the fire, and stirring a big pot.

"Good evening, missus," he says. "It's a fine evening."

"Yes," says she, and she went on stirring.

"Maybe it'll rain," he says, and he stood first on one foot and then on the other.

"Maybe," says she.

"And maybe it won't," he says, and looked out of the window.

"Maybe," says she.

And the fool scratched his head, and twisted round his hat.

43

"Well," says the fool, "I can't think of anything else to say about the weather, but let me see: the crops are getting on fine."

"Fine," says she.

"And . . . and . . . the beasts are fattening," he says.

"They are," says she.

"And . . . and . . ." he says, and he came to a stop. "I'll reckon we'll get down to business now; we've done the polite bit. Have you got any brains for sale?"

"That depends," says she. "If you want king's brains, or soldier's brains, or schoolmaster's brains, I don't keep them."

"Heavens, no!" he says. "Just ordinary brains – fit for any fool – the same as everyone else around here. Just something common-like."

"Yes, then," says the wise woman. "I might manage that, if you're ready to help yourself."

"How can I do that, missus?" he says.

"Like this," says she, peering into her pot. "You bring me the heart of the thing you like best, and I'll tell you where to get your pitcher of brains."

"But," says the fool, scratching his head, "how can I do that?"

"That's not for me to say," the wise woman says. "Find out for yourself, my lad, unless you want to be a fool all your days. But you'll have to answer me a riddle so I can be sure you've brought me the right thing, and have got your brains about you. And now," says the wise woman, "I've something else to see to – so good day to you." And she carried the pot away with her into the back room.

So off went the fool to his mother, and he told her what the wise woman had said.

"And I reckon I'll have to kill that pig," he says, "for I like bacon fat more than anything."

"Then do it, my lad!" says his mother. "It will certainly

44

be a marvellous thing if you're able to buy a pitcher of brains, and look after yourself."

So the fool killed the pig; and next day off he went to the wise woman's cottage, and there she sat, reading in a great book.

"Good day, missus," he says. "I've brought you the heart of the thing I like best of all. I'll put it on the table here – it's wrapped in paper."

"Oh, yes?" says she, and she looked at him through her spectacles. "Tell me this, then: what runs without feet?"

The fool scratched his head, and thought, and thought, but he couldn't say.

"Go away!" says she. "You haven't found me the right thing yet. I've no brains for you today." And she banged the book shut, and turned her back.

Off went the fool to tell his mother. But when he got near the house, people came running out to tell him his mother was dying. And when he got in, his mother simply looked at him, and smiled, as if to say she could leave him with a quiet mind, since he'd got brains enough now to look after himself – and then she died.

So the fool sat down, and the more he thought about it, the worse he felt. He remembered how she'd nursed him when he was a little baby, and helped him with his lessons, and cooked his dinners, and mended his shoes, and put up with his foolishness, and he felt sorrier and sorrier, and began to sigh and sob.

"Oh, mother, mother!" he says. "Who'll take care of me now? You shouldn't have left me alone, for I liked you better than anything!"

As soon as he said that, the fool thought of the wise woman's words. "Hi, yi!" he says. "Have I got to cut out my mother's heart and take it to the wise woman? I don't like this job." And he took out a knife and tested its edge.

"No, I can't do it," says the fool. "What shall I do? What

shall I do to get that pitcher of brains now I'm alone in the world? So he thought and thought and then he went and borrowed a sack; he bundled his mother into it, and carried it on his shoulder up to the wise woman's cottage.

"Good day, missus," he says. "I reckon I've found you the right thing this time, and that's for sure." And he plumped the sack down kerflap! on the doorstep.

"Maybe," says the wise woman. "But now tell me this: what's yellow and shining but isn't gold?"

The fool scratched his head, and thought, and thought, but he couldn't say.

"Well! You haven't hit on the right thing, my lad," says she. "I do believe you're a bigger fool than I thought!" And she shut the door in his face.

"Look at me, then," says the fool, and he sat down by the roadside and sobbed. "I've lost the only two things I cared for, and what else can I find to buy a pitcher of brains with?" And with that, the fool fairly howled, until the tears ran down into his mouth.

Then up came a girl who lived nearby, and she looked at him. "What's up with you, fool?" says she.

"Oo! I've killed my pig, and lost my mother, and I'm nothing but a fool myself," he says between sobs.

"That's bad," she says. "And haven't you got anybody to look after you?"

"No," he says, "and I can't buy my pitcher of brains because there's nothing I like best left!"

"What are you talking about?" says she.

Then down she sat, next to the fool, and the fool told her all about the wise woman and the pig, and his mother and the riddles, and said he was alone in the world.

"Well!" says she, "I wouldn't mind looking after you myself."

"Could you manage?" he says.

"Oh, yes!" says she. "People say fools make good husbands, and I reckon I'll have you, if you're willing."

"Can you cook?" he says.

"Yes, I can," says she.

"And scrub?" he says.

"To be sure!" says she.

"And mend my shoes?" he says.

"I certainly can," says she.

"Then I reckon you'll do as well as anybody," the fool says. "But what shall I do about this wise woman?"

"Oh, wait a bit," says she. "Something may turn up. It doesn't matter whether you're a fool or not, as long as you've got me to look after you."

"That's true," he says. So off they went and got married.

The girl kept his house so clean and neat, and cooked him such tasty dinners, that one night the fool said to her. "Lass, I've been thinking I like you better than anything, when all's said and done."

"That's good to hear," says she. "And so?"

"Have I got to kill you, do you think, and take your heart up to the wise woman for the pitcher of brains?"

"Lord, no!" says the girl, looking scared. "I wouldn't do that. But see here: you didn't cut out your mother's heart, did you?"

"No. But if I had, maybe I'd have got my pitcher of brains." the fool says.

"Not a bit of it," says she. "Just you take me up as I am, heart and all, and I bet I can help you answer the riddles."

"Can you really?" the fool says, doubtfully.

"Well," says she, "let's see now. Tell me the first one."

"What runs without feet?" he says.

"Why, water!" says she.

"It does," the fool says, and he scratched his head. "And what's yellow and shining, but isn't gold?"

"Why, the sun!" says she.

"Faith, it is!" the fool says. "Come, let's go to the wise woman at once!" So off they went and, as they walked up the path, they saw her sitting at her door, twining straws.

"Good day, missus," the fool says.

"Good day, fool," says she.

"I reckon I've found you the right thing at last," he says. "I haven't exactly cut the heart out, though. It's such mucky work."

The wise woman looked at them both, and wiped her spectacles. "Can you tell me what has no legs at first, and then two legs, and ends up with four legs?"

The fool scratched his head, and thought, and thought, but he couldn't say.

Then the girl whispered in his ear: "It's a tadpole."

"Maybe," says the fool, "it might be a tadpole, missus."

The wise woman nodded her head. "That's right," says she, "and you've got your pitcher of brains already."

"Where are they?" the fool says, looking around, and feeling in his pockets.

"In your wife's head," says she. "The only cure for a fool is a good wife to look after him, and that you've got – so good day to you!" And with that she nodded to them, and stood up and went into her house.

So the fool and the girl went home together, and the fool never wanted to buy a pitcher of brains again, for his wife had enough for them both.

Sea Tongue

I am the bell. I'm the tongue of the bell. I was cast before your grandmother was a girl. Before your grandmother's grandmother. So long ago.

Listen now! I'm like to last. I'm gold and green, cast in bronze, I weigh two tons. Up here, in the belfry of this closed church, I'm surrounded by sounds. Mouthfuls of air. Words ring me.

High on this crumbling cliff, I can see the fields of spring and summer corn; they're green and gold, as I am. I can see the shining water, silver and black, and the far fisherman on it. And look! Here comes the bellringer – the old bellwoman.

I am the bellwoman. For as long as I live I'll ring this old bell for those who will listen.

Not the church people: they have all gone. Not the seabirds; not the lugworms; not the inside-out crabs nor the shining mackerel. Whenever storms shatter the glass or fogs take me by the throat, I ring for the sailor and the fisherman. I warn them off the quicksands and away from the crumbling cliff. I ring and save them from the sea-god.

I am the sea-god. My body is dark; it's so bright you can scarcely look at me, so deep you cannot fathom me.

My clothing is salt-free raised by the four winds, twisting shreds of mist, shining gloom. And fog, fog, proofed and damp and cold. I'll wrap them round the fisherman. I'll wreck his boat.

I remember the days when I ruled earth. I ruled her all – every grain and granule – and I'll rule her again. I'll gnaw at this crumbling cliff tonight. I'll undermine the church and its graveyard. I'll chew on the bones of the dead.

We are the dead. We died in bed, we died on the sword, we fell out of the sky, we swallowed the ocean.

To come to this: this green graveyard with its rows of narrow beds. Each of us separate and all of us one.

We lived in time and we're still wrapped in sound and movement – gull-glide, gull-swoop. We live time out, long bundles of bone bedded in the cliff.

I am the cliff. Keep away from me. I'm jumpy and shrinking, unsure of myself. I may let you down badly.

Layers and bands, boulders and gravel and grit and little shining stones: these are earth's bones. But the sea-god keeps laughing and crying and digging and tugging. I scarcely know where I am and I know time is ending.

Fences. Red flags. Keep away from me. I'm not fit for the living.

We are the living. One night half of a cottage – Peter's cottage – bucketed down into the boiling water and he was left standing on the cliff-edge in his night-shirt.

After that, everyone wanted to move inland. We had no choice. You've only to look at the cracks. To listen to the sea-god's hollow voice!

Every year he comes closer. Gordon's cottage went down.

And Martha's. And Ellen's. The back of the village became the front. And now what's left? Only the bellwoman's cottage, and the empty shell of the church.

I am the church.

I remember the days when the bellows wheezed for the organ to play. I remember when people got down on their knees and prayed.

I've weathered such storms. Winds tearing at the walls, flint-and-brick, salt winds howling.

And now, tonight, this storm. So fierce, old earth herself is shaking and shuddering. Ah! Here comes the old bellwoman.

I am the bellwoman. There! Those lights, stuttering and bouncing. There's a boat out there, and maybe ten.

Up, up these saucer steps as fast as I can. Up!

Here in this mouldy room, I'll ring and ring and ring, and set heaven itself singing, until my palms are raw. I'll drown the sea-god.

I am the sea-god. And I keep clapping my luminous hands.

Come this way, fisherman, over the seal's bath and here along the cockle-path. Here are the slick quicksands, and they will have you.

Fisherman, come this way over the gulls' road and the herring-haunt! Here, up against this crumbling cliff. Give me your boat.

I am the boat. To keep afloat; to go where my master tells me: I've always obeyed the two commandments.

Now my master says forward but the sea-god says back; my master says anchor but the night-storm says drag. My deck is a tangle of lines and nets and ropes; my old heart's heavy with sluicing dark water. I'm drowning; I'm torn apart.

Groan and creak: I quiver; I weep salt. Shouts of the fishermen. Laughter of the sea-god. Scream of the night-storm.

I am the night-storm. I AM THE STORM.

Down with the bell and down with the belfry. Down on the white head of the bellwoman. Down with the whole church and the tilting graveyard. Down with the cliff itself, cracking and opening and sliding and collapsing. Down with them all into the foam-and-snarl of the sea.

I'm the night-storm and there will be no morning.

I am the morning. I am good morning.

My hands are white as white doves, and healing. Let me lay them on this purple fever. Let them settle on the boat. Nothing lasts for ever. Let me give you back your eyes, fisherman.

I am the fisherman. I heard the bell last night. Joe and Grimus and Pug, yes we all did! I heard the bell and dropped anchor. But there is no bell. There's no church, there's no belfry along this coast. Where am I? Am I dreaming?

Well! God blessed this old boat and our haul of shiners. He

saw fit to spare us sinners. We'll take our bearings, now, and head for home.

But I heard the bell. And now! I can hear it! Down, down under the boat's keel. I can hear the bell.

I am the bell. I am the tongue of the bell, gold and green, far under the swinging water.

I ring and ring, in fog and storm, to save boats from the quicksands and the rocky shore. I'm like to last; I'm cast in bronze, I weigh two tons.

Listen now! Can you hear me. Can you hear the changes of the sea?

The Strangers' Share

‥•————◆————•‥

Have you heard about the Strangers? Who? The Strangers.

There used to be heaps of them around; yes, and there still are. Do I really believe in them? Have I seen one? Yes, that I have. I've seen them often. I saw one only last spring.

The marshmen and marshwomen mainly call them the Strangers or else Little People, because they're no bigger than newborn babies. Or else they call them Greencoaties, because they wear green jackets; or sometimes the Earthkin, because they live in the earth. But mainly the Strangers, because that's what they are: strange in their looks and habits, strange in their likes and dislikes, and strangers amongst the marsh people.

They're very little creatures, no more a span from top to toe, with arms and legs as thin as thread, but great big feet and hands, and heads rolling around on their shoulders.

They wear grass-green jackets and breeches, and have yellow bonnets on their heads, for all the world like toadstools. Their faces are strange, with long noses, and wide mouths, and great red tongues hanging out and flap-flapping about.

I've never heard one talk, I don't think. But when they're upset about anything, they grin and yelp like angry hounds, and when they feel merry and cuddlesome, they twitter and cheep as softly and sweetly as the little birds.

When I was a boy, and my grandfather was a boy, the Strangers showed themselves more often than now, and people weren't as afraid of them as you'd have thought. If they were crossed, they were mischievous angry things, but provided they were left alone they didn't harm anyone or meddle with anybody's business. And if people were good to them, they never forgot it, and would do anything to help them out in return.

On summer nights, they danced in the moonlight on the great flat stones you see lying around here. I don't know where the stones came from, but my grandfather told me his grandfather told him that, long ago, the marsh people used to light fires on the stones, and smear them with blood, and thought a lot more about the Strangers than about the parson and the church.

And on winter nights, when people were in bed, the Strangers would dance in the hearth; and the crickets played for them for all they were worth.

Yes, the Strangers were always in the thick of things. At harvest time, they pulled at the ears of corn, and tumbled amongst the stubble, and wrestled with the poppy-heads. And in the year's spring, they were busy shaking and pinching the leafbuds and blossom-buds on the trees, to open them, and tweaking the buds of flowers, and chasing the butterflies, and tugging the worms out of the earth. They were always playing around like tomfools, but they were happy and no worse than mischievous so long as they weren't crossed. You had only to stay mum and keep still as death and you'd see the busy little things running and playing all round you.

The marsh people knew the Strangers helped the corn to ripen, and all the green things to grow; and knew they painted the pretty colours of the flowers, and the reds and browns of the fruit in autumn, and the yellowing leaves. Then they thought how, if the Strangers got upset, all the green things would dwindle and wither, and the harvest would fail, and everyone would go hungry. So they did everything they could think of to please the little people, and to stay friends with them.

In each garden, the first flowers and the first fruit, and the first cabbage or whatever, would be taken to the nearest flat stone, and laid there for the Strangers. In the fields, the first ears of corn, or the first potatoes, were given to the little people. And in each home, before people sat to eat, a bit of bread and a drop of milk or beer was spilled into the fireplace, in case the Greencoaties were hungry or thirsty.

But as time went by, the marsh people grew sort of careless. Maybe they went more to church and thought less about the Strangers, and the customs of their fathers; maybe they forgot the old tales their grandfathers had told them; or maybe they thought they'd grown so wise that they knew better than all the generations before them.

Anyhow, and however it happened, the flat stones of the Strangers stayed bare; the first fruits of the earth were withheld, and people sat to their food without sparing a crumb for the fireplace. The little people were left to look after themselves, and to hunger and thirst if they wanted to.

I reckon the Strangers couldn't make it out at first. I don't know, maybe they talked it over amongst themselves. For a long time, though, they kept quiet and never showed they were upset with the marsh people's unfriendly ways. Perhaps to begin with they just couldn't believe people would grow so careless about the Earthkin – after all, they'd been good neighbours to the marshmen and marshwomen for longer than I can tell. But as time went on, they couldn't help but see the truth of it, for people got worse and worse every day. Yes, and they took the very stones of the Strangers from the fields and the sides of lanes, and threw them away.

So it went on, and the marsh children grew up to be men and women, and scarcely knew a thing about the little people who had been such friends of their parents and grandparents. And the old folk had almost completely forgotten about them.

But the Strangers hadn't forgotten – no! they remembered

the earlier times only too well, they did, and they were only waiting for a good chance to pay back the marsh people for their bad manners. And at last it came. It was slow to come – just as the marsh people were slow to forget their regard for the little people; but it was sure – it was sure as hell-fire.

Summer after summer the harvest failed, and the green things dwindled, and the animals fell sick. Summer after summer the crops came to nothing, and the marsh fever got worse, and children sickened and died, and whatever the marsh people put their hands to went wrong and arsy-versy.

Summer after summer things were like this, until the marsh people lost heart, and instead of working in the fields they sat on their doorsteps, or by their fires, waiting for better luck to come their way. But better luck never came near them – not a glimpse of it! Food became scarce, children moaned for hunger, and babies wasted away.

And when the fathers looked at their wives, with their dead babies at their breasts, and turned their hollowed eyes from the sickly children who moaned for bread, what could they do but drink until they were merry, and their troubles forgotten until next day? In time, some of the women consoled themselves in the same way, while others took to stuffing themselves stupid with opium, whenever they could get hold of it, and the children died all the faster. Everything was so terrible that the people thought it was the Day of Judgement, and the beginning of hell itself.

But one day the wise women met together; and they did the dreadful things they never talk about, and with fire and blood they discovered the truth of it. Then they tramped through the little marsh hamlets and into the yards, and into the inns, and up and down the whole shire, and they called on the marsh people to meet them next evening as soon as it grew dark. And the people wondered and scratched their heads, but the next night they all came to the meeting-place by the crossroads to listen to the wise women.

Then the wise women told them everything they'd found out.

"The Strangers are working against us, and meddling with everything," said one wise woman. "They're meddling with our crops and our animals, and with our babies and children. Our only chance is to make it up with the little people."

"Our parents and our grandparents and the generations before them used to keep friendly with the Strangers," said another wise woman. "They gave them the first fruits of the field and the first fruits of the garden. They gave them food. But in the end they stopped all that kind of thing, and pretty well turned their backs on the Greencoaties."

"The little people have been very patient," said the third wise woman. "They've waited, and waited for a long time, to see if we'd return to the old ways. But at last the time came to pay us all back, and so trouble and bad times have come to the marsh, as you all know."

"I call on every man who has seen his animals starving," said the first wise woman, "and on every man who has seen some job going arsy-versy."

"I call on every woman," said the second, "who has heard her children sob for bread, and had none to give them, and has buried her poor little baby before it was even out of her arms."

"Do as your parents and grandparents used to do," said the third wise woman. "Tell the old stories, listen to the old stories, make friends again with the little people! Get this curse lifted from you!"

Before long, the marshmen were shaking hands on the wise women's words, and the women were sobbing as they thought of the dead babies and hungry children – and they all went home to do their best to put the wrong right.

Well! I can't tell you everything, but as the curse of the Strangers came, so it went: slowly, slowly, the bad luck got better. The little people were upset, and the old times weren't to be won back in one day or even one summer. But first fruits were laid on the flat stones – wherever the stones could be found; and bread and drink were spilled on the hearth, as they used to be, and the old people told the children all the old stories, and taught them to believe them and to give time and thought to the bogles and boggarts and the green-coated Strangers.

And slowly, slowly, the little people stopped being angry. They got on with the marsh people again, and lifted the curse they had laid upon them. And slowly, slowly, the harvest got better, and the animals got fatter, and the children held up their heads; but for all that, it wasn't the same as it used to be.

The marsh men took to gin and the women to their opium; they were always shaken by fevers, and the children were yellow and puny. Times were better, and people did well enough, and the Strangers weren't at all unfriendly, but things were still not as gay as before the evil days, when the marsh people hadn't known what it was to go hungry and thirsty – and before the churchyard was so full with the little graves, and cradles in people's homes sometimes rocked dead children.

Ah! And all this came of turning from the old ways. I reckon it's best to keep to them, in case bad luck should be sent as payment for bad manners.

The Spectre of Wandlebury

Sir Osbert Fitzhugh and his squire rode down the spine of England. They rode south from the Border over the moors, under the peaks, into the heart, around the fens, and at last they reached Cambridge Castle.

"I'm in search of wonders," Sir Osbert told his ancient host, as they sat at the fire.

"All around us," the old man said. "And all too many. Boggarts and bogles, and dead hands in the fen, woodwoses and phantoms . . ."

"Tell me more," said Osbert, and his bushy brown eyebrows twitched.

"And the nearest wonder is the greatest."

Osbert's squire glanced over his shoulder, and to his eyes the whole gloomy hall looked mysteriously alive: alive in the fire-light with spectres and memories and dancing shadows.

"Wandlebury," said the host. "Have you heard of it?"

The fire crackled and spat.

"There's an old earth-fort near here. Wandlebury. If you enter it alone under the full moon, and shout 'Knight to knight! Show yourself!'"

"What then?" asked Osbert.

"Then a knight will appear out of the darkness. Out of air! A spectre! He's mounted and fully armed – and ferocious. He'll joust with his challenger and hurl him to the ground."

"And if the challenger throws the spectre?" asked the squire.

The ancient host looked at the eager young squire. "That has never happened," he said.

For a while the three of them sat in silence in front of the licking, sucking, swallowing, biting, spitting fire.

"Alone," said the old man again. "You have to go in to the earth-fort alone. Through the three ramparts. Your companions can wait and watch outside."

"Full moon," said Osbert thoughtfully, and then he vigorously rubbed both his eyebrows. "All right! I'll challenge him."

"Seventy-six years," cried the host, and his head shook. "In all my long lifetime, no one has dared it."

"Who risks nothing wins nothing," said Osbert.

"They say the old gods are buried up there," the old man said. "Up there on the hillside where earth and sky meet."

The moon was clean and acute; the stars were like sky-gorse.

Sir Osbert and his squire clattered over the moat and rode away to the south-east. First they followed an old track, then they galloped out onto the Gogmagog Hills, and the gloomy ramparts of Wandlebury reared up in front of them.

Just in front of the entrance – a gap in the earth-walls – the two riders reined in.

"Remember our host's words!" Osbert said. "Alone! And you must wait here."

The squire nodded.

Osbert stared at the hill-fort and then he put his right hand on the squire's shoulder. He seemed to be on the very point of saying something but perhaps he thought better of it, for abruptly he dug in his heels, broke into a canter, and entered the fort.

It was very still inside the waiting ramparts. Watchful. Waiting. Chill and almost airless.

Osbert looked about him. Then slowly he rode right round the inside of the fort, and the moon's face shone so brightly that he could see every molehill.

When Osbert had completed the circuit, he drew up,

pulled off his gauntlets and put his mouth to his knuckles and fists and blew on them.

"All right!" he said in a low voice. And then much louder: "All right!"

Sir Osbert Fitzhugh walked his horse to the centre of the fort. There he raised his lance and shook it at the moon, and then he shouted out, "Knight to knight! Show yourself!"

Things happened exactly as the old host said they would.

First there came a whinny and a snort. And then, out of the darkness, out of air, as if he were made of them, there rode a knight – a knight or whatever he was. He rode right up to Sir Osbert.

Under the steely light of the moon, Osbert looked at him: his sombre armour and death-dark shield, his superb jet-black mount with its charcoal trappings. Osbert looked and he knew that, behind his closed visor, the Knight of Wandlebury was looking at him.

"Will you fight?" he asked, and he licked his lips. "Will you joust?"

By way of reply, the figure couched its lance and rode away to the far side of the fort. Osbert couched his lance, too, and walked his nervous horse in the opposite direction. Then both knights wheeled round and at once galloped back towards each other.

Their armour clinked and rang; their leather straps and saddles creaked and groaned; the hooves of their mounts pounded, pounded on the ground.

But try as he would, Osbert was unable to balance his lance; and when the two knights met, its gleaming tip was still pointing at Orion, the shining hunter. The Knight of Wandlebury's aim was fearsome, though. His lance grazed Osbert's left cheek-guard – it was within an inch of staving in his visor or crushing his windpipe.

When they tilted at each other for a second time, neither knight was able to hit the other, and their two horses careered away into the darkness. But at the third end, Osbert was the more skilful. He drove his lance against his opponent's breast-bone, just under the heart, and the dark knight was thrown right over his horse's crupper.

At once, Osbert galloped after the riderless black horse. Round and round the inside of the earth-fort he chased it, until he was able to grab its bridle.

"I claim him!" roared Osbert. "I claim him!"

The Knight of Wandlebury slowly got on to his hands and knees – his feet. He began to stagger towards Osbert and then, fully armed as he was, he broke into a kind of run.

Osbert saw he had drawn a short spear and, without letting go of the black horse's bridle, he laid his right hand on his sword hilt. It was of no use, though. He had not even unsheathed it before the dark knight raised his flashing spear and flung it at Osbert.

Osbert felt a savage stab of pain just under his right hip. He screwed up his eyes. And when he opened his eyes again, the dark knight had vanished. Into the darkness. Into air.

Still mounted, Sir Osbert slowly led the magnificent horse out of the earth-fort, and at the entrance his squire was waiting for him.

"Where did he go?" gasped Osbert. "Did you see which way?"

"He vanished, sire," said the squire. "In the winking of an eye. He just vanished."

"On foot!" said Osbert, with some satisfaction.

"Yes, sire,"

"Leaving this splendid beast behind him."

"Are you hurt, sire?" asked the squire.

"Nothing," said Osbert. "Almost nothing. Warm water. Wine."

"You are hurt," said the squire, and gently he took the bridle of the black horse from Osbert's left hand. "Let me lead him back to the Castle."

Sir Osbert Fitzhugh and his squire rode down off the Gogmagog Hills. They followed the old track north and west and, a few minutes before cockcrow, they clattered over the moat into the courtyard of Cambridge Castle.

There they tethered the black horse and their own mounts. Then the squire put one hand under Sir Osbert's right shoulder, and helped him up the lamplit stairs into the great hall.

To their surprise, their ancient host was still sitting in his great oak chair beside the fire. He had waited up for them through the watches of the night and, when he heard their foot-steps, he roused himself, rubbed his eyelids and stretched. His face was pink and scrubbed, and as unlined as a baby's.

"You fought with him," the old man said. "You fought with the spectre."

Sir Osbert Fitzhugh inclined his head, and then he staggered sideways.

"Sire," said the squire. "He was wounded. He is hurt."

"Sit here, man," said the host, guiding Osbert to his own seat by the fire.

Then the squire unlaced the greave covering Osbert's right leg, and when he took off his metal boot, he saw the blood swilling around in it.

"Never mind that!" said Osbert. "Water! Wine! I want you to see the black horse."

"The black horse!" exclaimed the old man.

"The Knight of Wandlebury's horse," said the squire.

"Everyone must see this wonder," said the host. "Wait here! Let me wake my servants. They can sleep another night."

Sir Osbert and his squire and their ancient host led the way down to the courtyard, and a tumble of grumbling, groaning servants followed them. They were all wearing nightshirts, and were wrapped in woollen blankets, hempen sacks, animal skins – anything to keep out the dawn-cold.

Then the grumbling and groaning stopped. Everyone marvelled at the magnificent black horse, and one of the grooms reckoned he was at least eighteen hands high. In the first light, more grey than green, more green than blue, they could all see his glossy coat and mane and tail were raven-black. And they saw the look in his rolling eyes – fierce and almost wild.

But then the cock crew, and the moment it did so, the black horse reared up on its tether, and its eyes rolled terribly. It snorted and whinnied, and stamped on the ground. Sparks like fallen stars danced around its hooves. Then it reared up again, right over the watching crowd, and snapped its tether.

At once the black horse galloped out of the castle courtyard. The ancient host tottered afer it, and the squire and many of the servants ran after it, but no – they couldn't catch up with it. They couldn't even see it. It had vanished into the vanishing night.

In the castle, wise women applied salves and poultices to Sir Osbert's thigh-wound. Days passed, like cloud-shadows racing over the fields, and at last the knight and his squire took leave of their ancient host. They rode north, around the fen, into the heart, under the peaks, over the moors. They rode up the spine of England and at last they reached the Border.

But every year, for as long as he lived, on the same night he had jousted with the spectre, Sir Osbert's thigh-wound burst open. It oozed, it bled and filled his right shoe with blood.

"A proof," said Osbert. "And a warning. And after I die, let some man use blood-bright words. Let him write down how I jousted with the Spectre of Wandlebury."

What a Donkey!

····•——◆▸—•····

There were three students at Cambridge who worked a little, and talked a lot, and never had any money.

"We haven't even got enough to buy supper," said the first.

"We're asses if we can't think how to get some," said the second. "What did God give us brains for?"

"Would you rather be poor and clever or rich and stupid?" said the third student (whose friends called him Ned).

So the three students went out walking the streets of Cambridge, looking for a way to lay their hands on some money.

In the street leading to the market, they saw a donkey, with a handsome broad black stripe across its shoulders and a bushy tuft at the end of its tail, tethered to the handle of a cottage door.

"All right!" said Ned, the third student. "I've got an idea."

At once he bent down, untied the donkey's girth and lifted off its two empty baskets.

"What are you doing?" said the first student.

"Quick!" said Ned. "Take off his bridle! Yes! And now put them on me. Put the bridle on my head. And the baskets on my back."

"What for?" said the second student.

"Untie the halter," said Ned.

"Why?" said the first student.

"Now get that donkey away as fast as you can," said Ned.

"Sell it in the market! I'll meet you there as soon as I can."

"Right!" said the first student and "Right!" said the second student. And they hurried away with the donkey as fast as they could.

Before long, the donkey's owner came out of the little cottage, where he had been smoking a quiet pipe and drinking a pint of beer. He wasn't a rich man or a clever one; he was a tinker.

"What the devil's this?" he shouted, when he saw Ned with the baskets on his back, and the donkey's bit between his teeth. "What's going on?"

"Excuse me, sir," said Ned. "I'll try to explain."

"Who are you?" said the tinker.

"That's the point," said Ned. "Seven years ago I had a terrible argument with my father. A terrible argument, and he turned me into a donkey."

"A donkey," said the tinker.

"And for seven years," said Ned, "I've been kicked and cursed, and I've carried loads. You were my only kind owner."

"Dear God!" said the poor man.

"But now, at long last, the seven years are over. They're over today, and you must set me free."

"Of course! Of course!" said the tinker untying the girth and lifting away the two empty baskets, and then taking off the bridle-head-stall and reins and bit.

"Thank goodness for that!" said Ned, giving himself a shake.

"What's your name, then?" said the poor man.

"Duncan," said the third student. "Duncan. My friends call me Ned." And with that, the student shook hands with the poor man, and thanked him, and ran off down the street towards the market. But when he was safely out of earshot, he just threw back his head and brayed with laughter.

Poor as he was, the tinker decided he would have to buy

another donkey, so that he could travel his odds and ends from fair to fair. Only a few days later, he walked ten miles to a nearby fair, and made his way straight to the animal pens. There were several donkeys for sale there and, much to his surprise, the tinker immediately recognised one of them: there was no mistaking that handsome broad black stripe across its shoulders and the bushy tuft at the end of its tail.

When the donkey saw the tinker, it recognised him too, and began to bray. How mournfully it brayed, as if it were begging its owner to buy it back!

But the tinker would have none of it. "So you've quarrelled with your father again, have you?" he said. "Already! Well, dang me if I'll buy you for a second time."

Samuel's Ghost

Poor little Samuel! He was asleep when his cottage caught fire, and when he woke up it was too late. He was only a lad and he was burned to death; he got turned into ashes, and maybe cinders.

After a while, though, Samuel got up. The inside of him got up and gave itself a shake. He must have felt rather queer: he wasn't used to doing without a body, and he didn't know what to do next, and all around him there were boggarts and bogles and chancy things, and he was a bit scared.

Before long, Samuel heard a voice. "You must go to the graveyard," said whatever it was, "and tell the Big Worm you're dead,"

"Must I?" said Samuel.

"And ask him to have you eaten up," said the something. "Otherwise you'll never rest in the earth."

"I'm willing," said Samuel.

So Samuel set off for the graveyard, asking the way, and rubbing shoulders with all the horrid things that glowered around him.

By and by, Samuel came to an empty dark space. Glimmering lights were crossing and recrossing it. It smelt earthy, as strong as the soil in spring, and here and there it gave off a ghastly stink, sickening and scary. Underfoot were creeping things, and all round were crawling, fluttering things, and the air was hot and tacky.

On the far side of this space was a horrid great worm, coiled up on a flat stone, and its slimy head was nodding and swinging from side to side, as if it were sniffing out its dinner.

Samuel was afraid when he heard something call out his name, and the worm shot its horrid head right into his face.

"Samuel! Is that you, Samuel? So you're dead and buried, and food for the worms, are you?"

"I am," said Samuel.

"Well!" said the worm. "Where's your body?"

"Please, your worship," said Samuel – he didn't want to anger the worm, naturally – "I'm all here!"

"No," said the worm. "How do you think we can eat you? You must fetch your corpse if you want to rest in the earth."

"But where is it?" said Samuel, scratching his head. "My corpse?"

"Where is it buried?" said the worm.

"It isn't buried," said Samuel. "That's just it. It's ashes. I got burned up."

"Ha!" said the worm. "That's bad. That's very bad. You'll not taste too good."

Samuel didn't know what to say.

"Don't fret," said the worm. "Go and fetch the ashes. Bring them here and we'll do all we can."

So Samuel went back to his burned-out cottage. He looked and looked. He scooped up all the ashes he could find into a sack, and took them off to the great worm.

Samuel opened the sack, and the worm crawled down off the flat stone. It sniffed the ashes and turned them over and over.

"Samuel," said the worm after a while. "Something's missing. You're not all here, Samuel. Where's the rest of you? You'll have to find the rest."

"I've brought all I could find," said Samuel.

"No," the worm said. "There's an arm missing."

"Ah!" said Samuel. "That's right! I lost an arm I had."

"Lost?" asked the worm.

"It was cut off," said Samuel.

"You must find it, Samuel."

Samuel frowned. "I don't know where the doctor put it," he said. "I can go and see."

So Samuel hurried off again. He hunted high and low, and after a while he found his arm.

Samuel went straight back to the worm. "Here's the arm," he said.

The worm slid off its flat stone and turned the arm over.

"No, Samuel," said the worm. "There's something still missing. Did you lose anything else?"

"Let's see," said Samuel. "Let's see . . . I lost a nail once, and that never grew again."

"That's it, I reckon!" said the worm. "You've got to find it, Samuel!"

"I don't think I'll ever find that, master," said Samuel. "Not one nail. I'll give it a try though."

So Samuel hurried off for the third time. But a nail is just as hard to find as it's easy to lose. Although Samuel searched and searched, he couldn't find anything; so at last he went back to the worm.

"I've searched and searched and I've found nothing," said Samuel. "You must take me without my nail – it's no great loss, is it? Can't you make do without it?"

"No," said the worm. "I can't. And if you can't find it – are you quite certain you can't, Samuel?"

"Certain, worse luck!"

"Then you must walk! You must walk by day and walk by night. I'm very sorry for you, Samuel, but you'll have plenty of company!"

Then all the creeping things and crawling things swarmed round Samuel and turned him out. And unless he has found it, Samuel has been walking and hunting for his nail from that day to this.

The Devil Take the Hindmost

⋯•———◆———•⋯

"Midnight, then," said Mace. George Mace. He glared at his two companions, and then sniffed and drank off the rest of his beer, "Breckles Hall. You know where."

Almost at once two more men got up from a table on the other side of the bar, and sauntered over to him. As if he were a magnet and they were two poor pins.

"Midnight," repeated Mace. "The Hall. You know where." He stood up and stretched, like a giant bat reaching right over them. "And the devil take the hindmost," he added. Slowly he coiled a piece of snaring-wire round the lowest button of his greatcoat. Then he walked out into the January night, who knows where.

The four men looked at one another and looked into their glasses of beer.

"The devil take the hindmost," muttered one man.

"He can go to the devil," another man said. "Mace."

"That's what he deserves," the third man said.

"And that's what he'll get," said the fourth.

There was something dark and chancy about Mace. He was deep as drowning water and dangerous as thin ice.

"You never know where you stand with him."

"He'll mother a stray kitten."

"And stab his own mother."

That's what people said.

Everyone in Watton muttered and complained about Mace behind his back, but no one criticised him to his face. No one crossed him or riled him; no, they did as he ordered them, because they were afraid of what might happen otherwise. No one walked alone with Mace, though, not since he and Bobby Cossey had gone out shooting near the sandpits, and only Mace had come back.

Mace's companions were nervous about their night's work, and they were uneasy about Breckles Hall – they knew about the phantom coach and its dark driver; and they'd heard about the Catholic priests in cramped priestholes, the Protestants with burning eyes and burning brands, ferreting them out; miserable suicides; and a mad woman entombed upright inside one wall. But the truth is, the four men were even more nervous of their leader. Each left his cottage in good time and they were all wearing sombre clothing: midnight blue jerseys, charcoal jackets, moleskin trousers, dun coats with wide pockets – nothing that could wink at the moon.

One man was carrying a snare, and another a grinning ferret; one had a couple of flams – little purse-nets; the fourth was carrying on his shoulder an ugly-looking trap; and each man had a hempen sack.

Mace was waiting for them under the great oak in the middle of the little wood in front of Breckles Hall.

"That's a shiny night," said one man with satisfaction.

Mace gave a kind of nod – an upward thrust of his chin. "They're thumping in their burrows," he said.

Midnight and the wood was far from silent, for those with ears to hear such things. The poachers put their heads to the ground and listened to the rabbits running around their warrens. They heard the creak-creak of the pheasant and the oo-hoo of the barn owl. Mace was so sharp he could have heard a hare pricking up its ears.

"Now then," he said. "Two and two. I'll work on my own."

"Fred and me," said one man. "The old team."

"Who's running this show?" said Mace quietly.

The four men murmured.

"You all got wire?'

Again the men murmured.

"Right!" Laddie and Bill, you do the pheasants and the partridge. Fred! You and Martin do rabbit and hare. Yes, and the devil and I . . ." Mace stared at each of the four men in turn. "Right!" he said. "Five o'clock we'll meet in the gardener's shed – you know, behind the Hall."

"Five o'clock," said the men.

"And settle up," said Mace, "before the moon goes down. Five o'clock. And the devil take the hindmost."

That was a fine night's work. One of the very best. Pheasants and partridges and rabbits and hares! They fell into the flams and snares as if there were no tomorrow. And for them that did, there wasn't!

By five o'clock, Laddie and Bill and Fred and Martin had so much game in their sacks they could scarcely carry them to the shed behind the Hall. Indeed, Bill dragged his behind him, and it scored a track through the shining hoar-frost.

But where was Mace? Where was he?

"That's not like him," muttered Bill. "Not at all, that isn't."

The four men huddled in the shed. Inside was even colder than outside, and for the first time that night Jack Frost attacked them. He crept in and tweaked their noses; he pinched the lobes of their ears, and pincered their fingertips and nipped their toes. Then he showed his white teeth.

The moon sank. Jaundiced and weary, it hung on the skyline, and at last it disappeared. Then the darkness was intense. It was as if you could touch it. The kind of darkness that makes a man wonder what shape he is, and even whether he exists.

"What shall we do?" said one man in a low voice.

"Damn him!"

"Come on! Let's settle up!"

"Listen!" said Fred. "Listen!"

First it was no sound – only the sound of not-silence – and they couldn't tell what it was. Then it was distant, a very distant roaring, like a sound in your memory. Then it grew closer and began to rumble, but not like thunder. Not as grand as that. Closer, then, and as the men felt their sweat cold on the backs of their necks the sound rolled and crunched and cracked and spat. Coach wheels slowly rolling over gravel, rolling up to the front of the Hall.

The four poachers peered through the door of the shed, and saw swinging lights in the back windows of the Hall.

"That's them coach-lamps," muttered Fred. "Shining in at the front and out through the back."

That's just what it was. And now the lamps stopped swinging and the stained glass in the Hall's back windows threw patterns and patches of colour out across the frosty lawn in front of the poachers. Freezing blue. Grey-green, sickly as dawn. Scarlet, bright as rabbits' blood.

A creek and then a thump.

"That's the steps," Laddie whispered.

Another creak. And then silence – forever silence. And then the slam of the coach door.

The four men listened for the coach to roll away again. The sound of a voice; a whip, maybe; then hooves; and the cracking and crunching.

But there was not a sound. The lamps went out. And the coach vanished. If any of the men had been in the shed on his own, he would have thought he'd imagined it all.

"Home!" said Laddie hoarsely.

"Each man his own sack!"

As the men hurried to get home before dawn, they kept wondering about Mace. Where he was. What had happened to him. What to do about it. And they thought again of all they knew about Breckles Hall.

Next morning, Mace was found. George Mace. He was

lying dead (where he had been left) on the doorstep of Breckles Hall. His body was not marked and his clothes were not bloodstained. His eyes were open and staring and glassy and cold.

The Wildman

Don't ask me my name. I've heard you have names. I have no name.

They say this is how I was born. A great wave bored down a river, and at the mouth of the river it ran up against a great wave of the sea. The coupled waves kicked like legs and whirled like arms and swayed like hips; sticks in the water snapped like bones and the seaweed bulged like gristle and muscle. In this way the waves rose. When they fell, I was there.

My home is water as your home is earth. I rise to the surface to breathe air, I glide down through the darkening rainbow. The water sleeks my hair as I swim. And when I stand on the sea-bed, the currents comb my waving hair; my whole body seems to ripple.

Each day I go to the land for food. I swim to the shore, I'm careful not be seen. Small things, mice, shrews, moles, I like them to eat. I snuffle and grub through the growth and undergrowth and grab them, and squeeze the warm blood out of them, and chew them.

Always before sunset I'm back in the tugging, chuckling, sobbing water. Then the blue darkness that comes down over the sea comes inside me too. I feel heavy until morning. If I stayed too long on the land I might be found, lying there, heavy, unable even to drag myself back to the water.

My friends are seals. They dive as I do, and swim as I do. Their hair is like my hair. I sing songs with their little ones.

They've shown me their secret place, a dark grotto so deep that I howled for the pain of the water pressing round me there and rose to the surface, gasping for air. My friends are the skimming plaice and the flickering eel and the ticklish trout. My friends are all the fishes.

As I swam near the river mouth, something caught my legs and tugged at them. I tried to push it away with my hands and it caught my hands and my arms too. I kicked; I flailed; I couldn't escape. I was dragged through the water, up out of the darkness into the indigo, the purple, the pale blue. I was lifted into the air, the sunlight, and down into a floating thing.

Others. There were others in it, others, others as I am. But their faces were not covered with hair. They had very little hair I could see except on their heads, but they were covered with animal skins and furs. When they saw me they were afraid and trembled and backed away and one fell into the water.

I struggled and bit but I was caught in the web they had made. They took me to land and a great shoal gathered round me there. Then they carried me in that web to a great high place of stone and tipped me out into a gloomy grotto.

One of them stayed by me and kept making noises; I couldn't understand him. I could tell he was asking me things. I would have liked to ask him things. How were you born? Why do you have so little hair? Why do you live on land? I looked at him, I kept looking at him, and when the others came back, I looked at them: their hairless hands, their legs, their shining eyes. There were so many of them almost like me, and I've never once seen anyone in the sea like me.

They brought me two crossed sticks. Why? What are they?

They pushed them into my face, they howled at me. One of them smacked my face with his hand. Why was that? It hurt. Then another with long pale hair came and wept tears over me. I licked my lips, the tears tasted like the sea. Was this one like me? Did this one come from the sea? I put my arms round its waist but it shrieked and pushed me away.

They brought me fish to eat. I wouldn't eat fish. Later they brought me meat; I squeezed it until it was dry and then I ate it.

I was taken out into sunlight, down to the river mouth. The rippling, rippling water. It was pink and lilac and grey; I shivered with longing at the sight of it. I could see three rows of webs spread across the river from bank to bank. Then they let me go, they let me dive into the water. It coursed through my long hair. I laughed and passed under the first web and the second web and the third web. I was free. But why am I only free away from those who are like me, with those who are not like me? Why is the sea my home?

They were all shouting and waving their arms, and jumping up and down at the edge of the water. They were all calling out across the grey wavelets. Why? Did they want me to go back after all? Did they want me to be their friend?

I wanted to go back, I wanted them as friends. So I stroked back under the webs again and swam to the sandy shore. They fell on me then, and twisted my arms, and hurt me. I howled. I screamed. They tied long webs round me and more tightly round me, and carried me back to the place of stone, and threw me into the gloomy grotto.

I bit through the webs. I slipped through the window bars. It was almost night and the blue heaviness was coming into me. I staggered away, back to the water, the waiting dark water.

A Coggeshall
Calendar

----◆----

It was April and the good people of Coggeshall were worried. Some of them were worried because there was too much wind, and some because there was too little.

"The black plague!" cried one old woman. "The wind keeps blowing it in."

And so she and her friends strung clothes-lines from tree to tree across the four roads leading into Coggeshall.

"The black plague!" cried the old women. "We must keep it out!"

Then they hung thick grey blankets over all the clothes-lines.

But the wind that worried the old women was not enough to please the two millers in the village.

"There's just not enough wind for us both," said one.

"We've got one mill too many," said the other. "That's the truth of it."

"You know what we must do?" the first miller said.

The two men walked and talked and, in the end, they shook hands and pulled down one of the mills.

It was July and the good people of Coggeshall were worried. Some of them were worried because it was not warm enough, and some because it was too wet.

"If we don't do something about it, there'll be no harvest this year," said one man.

"And what's more," said another, "we'll all get washed away."

So one group of villagers busied themselves in the

orchards, lighting bonfires under all the plum-trees to help the fruit to ripen.

But another group kept watch over the rising stream.

"It's about to break its banks."

"Remember what happened last time?"

"The flood, yes, the flood. Poor old Amy, she had to pull down her staircase."

"Otherwise the water would have got upstairs."

So they collected as many willow-hurdles and hazel-hurdles as they could, and put up a good, strong fence across the meadow between the stream and the village.

It was October and the good people of Coggeshall were worried because a rabid dog had bitten a wheelbarrow.

"That'll be the end of it," said one woman.

"It'll go mad," said her friend.

So the two of them hurriedly trundled the barrow into a garden shed, and chained it up, and locked it in.

It was December and the good people of Coggeshall were worried. All year they had been building a new church and everyone had lent a hand – man, woman and child. But they had forgotten to put in any windows.

"We'll have to do it the hard way," said the master-builder.

Hearing this, a large band of villagers went back to their homes in search of hampers and wheelbarrows – but not the barrow that was still in quarantine.

Back in the churchyard, they opened their hampers to catch the sunlight. Then, at a signal from the masterbuilder, they shut them up tight and wheeled them into the church.

When they opened their hampers again, and found no sunlight inside them, the villagers were very puzzled.

It was February and the good people of Coggeshall were

worried. They were worried because they had not built their fine new church in exactly the right place.

"There's nothing for it," said the masterbuilder. "We'll have to give it a push."

Freezing as it was, the masterbuilder and his companions all took off their coats and laid them on the ground outside the east end of the church. Then they went round to the west end and put their right shoulders against the rough wall.

"Ready!" said the masterbuilder.

Then they grunted and they shoved, and when they judged they had moved the church to its right position, they walked round to the east end again to pick up their coats.

But their coats had gone. Every single one of them.

"Darn!"

"Drat!"

"Where are they?"

"They can't have got up and walked away."

"You know what we've done," said the masterbuilder, pointing at the foot of the east wall. "What noodles we are! We've pushed the church right over them."

"Ah!" That's all right, then," said his companions, and they sighed in relief.

Then they all trooped into the church to collect their coats.

It was April and the good people of Coggeshall were worried. A whole year had passed by and they had not even noticed it. A whole year and it was time to begin again.

Cape of Rushes

There was once a very rich gentleman, and he had three daughters. He thought he'd see how fond of him they were, so he says to the first, "How much do you love me, my dear?"

"Why," says she, "I love you as much as I love my own life."

"That's good," he says. So he asks his second daughter, "How much do you love me, my dear?"

"Why," says she, "more than all the world."

"That's good," he says. So he asks his third daughter "How much do *you* love me, my dear?"

"Why," says she, "I love you as much as fresh meat loves salt," she says.

Well, the man was very angry. "You don't love me at all," he says, "and there's no room for you in this house." So he drove her out there and then, and shut the door in her face.

Well, the third daughter turned away, and she walked and walked until she came to a fen. And there she gathered a lot of rushes, and made them into a cape – a kind of cloak with a hood – to cover her from head to foot, and to hide her fine clothes. And then she walked on and on, until she came to a great house.

"Do you want a maid?" she says.

"No, we don't," they say.

"I've nowhere to go," she says, "and I'd ask no wages, and do any sort of work," says she.

"Well," they say, "if you want to wash the pots and scrape the saucepans, you can stay."

So there she stayed, and washed the pots and scraped the saucepans, and did all the dirty work. And because she never told them her name, they called her Cape of Rushes.

Well, one day there was to be a grand dance a little way away, and the servants were given time off to go and look at the fine people. Cape of Rushes said she was too tired to go, so she stayed at home.

But when the servants had gone, she threw off her cape of rushes, and cleaned herself up, and went to the dance. And no one there was so finely dressed as she.

Well, who should be there but her master's son? And what did he do but fall in love with her the minute he set eyes on her? He wouldn't dance with anyone else.

But before the dance was over, Cape of Rushes stepped off the floor, and away she went home. And when the other maids came back, she pretended to be asleep with her cape of rushes on.

Next morning, they said to her: "You did miss a sight, Cape of Rushes!"

"What was that?" says she.

"Why, the most beautiful lady you ever saw, marvellously dressed. The young master, he never took his eyes off her."

"Well, I should have liked to see her," says Cape of Rushes.

"Well, there's to be another dance this evening, and perhaps she'll be there."

But, come the evening, Cape of Rushes said she was too tired to go with them. When the servants had gone, though, she threw off her cape of rushes, and cleaned herself up, and away she went to the dance.

The master's son had been counting on seeing her. He danced with no one else, and never took his eyes off her.

But before the dance was over, she slipped away and home she went, and when the maids came back, she pretended to be asleep with her cape of rushes on.

Next day they said to her again: "Well, Cape of Rushes, you should have been there to see the lady. She was there again, looking marvellous, and the young master, he never took his eyes off her."

"Well, there," she says, "I should have liked to see her."

"Well," says they, "there's a dance again this evening, and you must come with us, for she's sure to be there."

When evening came, Cape of Rushes said she was too tired to go, and say what they would, she stayed at home. But when the servants had gone, she threw off her cape of rushes, and cleaned herself up and away she went to the dance.

The master's son was delighted when he saw her. He danced with no one but her, and never took his eyes off her. When she wouldn't tell him her name, or where she came from, he gave her a ring, and told her that if he didn't see her again he would die.

Well, before the dance was over, away she slipped, and home she went, and when the maids came home she was pretending to be asleep with her cape of rushes on.

Next day they said to her: "There, Cape of Rushes, you didn't come last night, and now you won't see the lady, for there are to be no more dances."

"Well, I'd very much have liked to see her," she says.

The master's son, he tried every way to find out where the lady had gone, but turn where he would, and ask whom he might, he couldn't find out a thing. And he became more and more ill because of his love for her, until he had to keep to his bed.

"Make some soup for the young master," they said to the cook. "He's dying for love of the lady." And the cook was just about to make it when Cape of Rushes came in.

"What are you doing there?" she says.

"I'm going to make some soup for the young master," says the cook, "because he's dying for love of the lady."

"Let me make it," says Cape of Rushes.

Well, the cook wouldn't let her at first, but at last she said yes; and Cape of Rushes made the soup. And when she had made it, she slipped the ring into it on the sly, before the cook took it upstairs.

The young man drank it, and saw the ring at the bottom.

"Send for the cook," he says. So the cook comes up.

"Who made this here soup?" he says.

The cook was frightened. "I did," she says. But then the young master looked at her.

"No, you didn't," he says. "Tell me who made it, and you'll come to no harm."

"Well, then, it was Cape of Rushes," says she.

So Cape of Rushes was called up.

"Did you make the soup?" he says.

"Yes, I did," says she.

"Where did you get this ring?" he says.

"From him who gave it to me," says she.

"Who are you, then?" says the young man.

"I'll show you," says she. And she threw off her cape of rushes, and there she was in her beautiful clothes.

Well, the master's son very soon got better, and he and Cape of Rushes were to be married not long after. It was to be a very grand wedding, and everyone was invited, from near and far. And Cape of Rushes' father was asked, but Cape of Rushes never told anyone who she really was.

But before the wedding she went to the cook, and she said, "I want you to prepare all the dishes without a grain of salt."

"They'll taste horrible," said the cook.

"That doesn't matter," she says.

"Very well," says the cook.

Well, the wedding day came, and they were married. And after the marriage, all the guests sat down to the wedding breakfast.

When they tried the meat, it was so tasteless they couldn't

eat it. Cape of Rushes' father tried first one dish and then another, and then he burst into tears.

"What's the matter?" asked the master's son.

"Oh!" says he, "I had a daughter. And I asked her how much she loved me. And she said, "As much as fresh meat loves salt." And I shut the door in her face, because I thought she didn't love me. And now I see she loved me best of all. And she may be dead for all I know."

"No, father, here she is," says Cape of Rushes.

And she goes up to him and puts her arms round him. And so they were happy ever after.

Sources and Notes

SHONKS AND THE DRAGON. *The History of Hertford-shire* by Nathaniel Salmon, London, 1728; *The Folklore of Hertfordshire* by Doris Jones-Baker, London, 1977; *Albion – A guide to Legendary Britain* by Jennifer Westwood, London, 1985.

The tombstone of Sir Piers Shonks lies in a recess in the north wall of the nave of Brent Pelham Church. And above it is a tablet with the inscription:

> Nothing of Cadmus nor St. George, those names
> Of great renown, survives them but their fames;
> Time was so sharp set as to make no Bones
> Of theirs, nor of their monumental Stones.
> But Shonks one serpent kills, t'other defies,
> And in this wall as in a fortress lies.

These lines, telling us that Shonks first killed a dragon and then outwitted the devil by having himself buried inside a wall (a motif that occurs in several British folk-tales) were probably written in the late 16th century. The tombstone, however, dates from the 13th century while Piers Shonks may well be one Peter Shank who lived in Brent Pelham in the 14th century. So we can say the legend as we know it today, combining two elements (dragon-slaying and tricking the devil), took shape between four and six hundred years ago.

To my ear, Shonks sounds a rather improbable name for a

dragon-slayer. So I've introduced a little humour into the story, and am also responsible for giving our hero a daughter and having her attend on Sir Piers when he fights the dragon.

LONG TOM AND THE DEAD HAND. 'The Dead Hand' in 'Legends of the Lincolnshire Cars' by Mrs M.C. Balfour in *Folk-Lore II, iii*, London, 1891.

Under the general headings of 'Legends of the Cars' and 'Legends of the Lincolnshire Cars' Mabel Balfour – a niece of Robert Louis Stevenson – printed nine astonishing Lincolnshire folk-tales in the journal *Folk-Lore* during 1891. I included three of them ('The Dead Moon', 'The Green Mist' and 'Yallery Brown') in my first collection of tales from East Anglia and the Fen Country, *The Dead Moon*, and have retold four more in this book. In each case, I have kept very close to the original but have modified the heavy Lincolnshire dialect.

In her foreword, Mrs Balfour writes that the Cars of the Ancholme valley "are still worth seeing, and have a beauty, or rather an attraction of their own. Stunted willows mark the dyke-sides, and in winter there are wide stretches of black glistening peat-lands and damp pastures; here and there great black snags work their way up from submerged forests below. When the mists rise at dusk in shifting wreaths, and the bleak wind from the North Sea moans and whistles across the valley, it is not difficult to people the Cars once more with all the uncanny dwellers, whose memory is preserved in the old stories."

TOM TIT TOT. *Ipswich Journal*, 15, 1878, contributed by Mrs A. Walter Thomas.

Mrs Walter Thomas says she heard this wonderful tale as a young girl from her old west Suffolk nurse. It is the English counterpart to the Grimms' tale of 'Rumpelstilzchen' (*Kinder-und-Hausmärchen*, 1812).

In his *English Fairy Tales*, Joseph Jacobs noted: 'One of the best folk-tales that have ever been collected, far superior to any Continental variants of this tale with which I am acquainted.'

THE GIPSY WOMAN. *East Anglian, VII*, 1897–8, contributed by Miss L.A. Fison and her sister Mrs A. Walter Thomas.

This tale, heard by the contributors from their nurse (see above) is a charming sequel to 'Tom Tit Tot' – and it's worth mentioning that the version of 'Tom Tit Tot' printed in *Merry Suffolk* (1899) ends with the words: 'Lork! How she did clap her hands for joy. "I'll warrant my master'll ha' forgot all about spinning next year," says she.'

THAT'S NONE OF YOUR BUSINESS. *Folk-Lore, III*, London, 1892, contributed by Lady Camilla Gurdon.

Lady Gurdon was told this snippet by her gardener and his wife, in south-east Suffolk.

A PITCHER OF BRAINS. 'A Pottle of Brains' in 'Legends of the Cars' by Mrs M.C. Balfour in *Folk-Lore II, ii*. London, 1891.

SEA TONGUE. 'The Undersea Bells' in *Forgotten Folk-Tales of the English Counties*, by Ruth Tongue, London, 1970.

The tale was collected from Norfolk fishermen in 1905 and 1928 by the Reverend John Tongue, who was at one time Vicar of Mundesley. The tale of a church bell or bells pealing under the water is common to several places along the Norfolk and Suffolk coast, including Dunwich, as well as to Cardigan Bay and the Lancashire coast.

I see my "fractured narrative" as a kind of sound-story for different voices (or for one voice taking the different parts). The form of the story – and this is the first time I've approached a folk-tale in this way – relates it to 'The Wildman', the other coastal tale in this collection, and owes something to the idea that everything in our universe, every stick and stone, has its own voice.

THE STRANGERS' SHARE. "Legends of the Lincolnshire Cars" by Mrs M.C. Balfour in *Folk-Lore, II, iii*, London, 1891.

At the heart of this important tale, which preserves many Lincolnshire beliefs and customs, lies a simple green message about respecting and cherishing the land that gives us life. The Strangers or Greencoaties are earth-spirits, just as Tiddy Mun, whose story I retold in *The Dead Moon*, is plainly the spirit of swamp and car and marsh and fen.

THE SPECTRE OF WANDLEBURY. *Otia Imperialia* by Gervase of Tilbury (ca. 1212 AD), edited by F. Liebrecht, Hanover, 1856.

The Iron Age hill-fort now known as Wandlebury Camp crowns the Gogmagog Hills near Stapleford in Cambridge-shire. Below it, there was once a hill-carving of a giant called Gogmagog (at one time a generic name for a giant), and maybe also more ancient carvings of long-forgotten gods. Furthermore, and rather confusingly, Lord Godolphin buried his Arab stallion in the Gogmagog Hills in the 18th century. But this burial has no connexion with our story, which dates from the early 13th century at the latest, while we simply do not know enough about the hill-carvings to relate them to the Knight of Wandlebury.

WHAT A DONKEY! 'The Metamorphosis' in *Facetiae Cantabrigienses*, London, 1825.

The theme of the thief who claims to have been changed into an ass or a donkey is common to the folk-tales of many European countries, including France and Spain, Holland and Germany, Lithuania, Italy and Hungary, and there is also a Philippine version of the story.

SAMUEL'S GHOST. 'Legends of the Lincolnshire Cars' by Mrs M.C. Balfour in *Folk-Lore II, iv*, London, 1891.

Mrs Balfour heard this funny-gruesome tale from Fanny, a crippled girl aged nine, who had heard it from her 'gran'. Fanny also told Mrs Balfour the story of 'The Dead Moon'.

Here, as in such stories as 'The Lambton Worm' and 'The Laidly Worm', the word 'worm' (derived from the Anglo-Saxon *wyrm*) means dragon.

THE DEVIL TAKE THE HINDMOST. *Highways and Byways of East Anglia* by William A. Dutt, London, 1904.

Like 'Shonks and the Dragon', this is a story with two elements: the death of a poacher and the appearance of a phantom coach. It is impossible to say when they first became connected.

In her splendid *Everyman's Book of English Folk Tales*, Sybil Marshall says that "Though the Devil is not specifically mentioned, one is left with the feeling that he certainly had some hand in the mysterious end of George Mace". I have developed this idea a little in the interests of dovetailing the two parts of the story.

This is one of several Norfolk tales describing the appearance of a phantom coach. Another tells how Anne Boleyn visits Blickling Hall (where she lived as a girl) every year on the night of her execution. Anne rides in a black hearse drawn by four headless horses; she is dressed in white and her own head lies in her lap.

Breckles Hall, once an Elizabethan manor and now a

farmhouse, lies three or four miles south-east of Watton, a small town midway between Thetford and East Dereham.

THE WILDMAN. *Chronicon Anglicanum* by Ralph (Radulphus) of Coggeshall (ca. 1210 AD).

Ralph was Abbot of the Cistercian monastery at Little Coggeshall from 1207–1218 (the inhabitants of Coggeshall are the subject of the next tale) near Colchester, and a lively chronicler of English history. He recorded two folk-tales. One concerns two green children, whose tale I retold in *The Dead Moon*, and who are the subject of Nicola LeFanu's and my opera, *The Green Children*. And the other concerns the wildman. Ralph tells us that a merman was caught by fishermen from Orford in Suffolk during the reign of Henry II (1154–89). He was completely naked, and covered in hair. He was imprisoned in the newly-built castle, did not recognise the Cross, did not talk despite torture, returned voluntarily into captivity after having eluded three rows of nets, and then disappeared never to be seen again.

A COGGESHALL CALENDAR. 'The Coggeshall Jobs' in *A Dictionary of British Folk-Tales* by Katharine M. Briggs, London, 1970–1.

No less than forty-five places in England are traditionally said to be inhabited by noodles or simpletons, including Gotham in Nottinghamshire (subject of the *Merie Tales of the Mad Men of Gotam*, published in the first half of the 16th century), Borrowdale in Westmoreland (Cumbria), St. Ives in Cornwall and the whole of the Isle of Wight! They all have light-hearted anecdotes similar to these (in some cases the same as these) told against them.

CAPE OF RUSHES. 'Cap o' Rushes' in *Ipswich Journal*. 1877, contributed by Mrs A. Walter Thomas.

Mrs Walter Thomas heard this tale as a child from an old

servant, in all likelihood the nurse who told her 'Tom Tit Tot' and 'The Gipsy Woman' (see above). It was originally called 'Cap o' Rushes'. But since it is clear that the teller meant by 'cap' a cloak with a hood, I have changed 'cap' to 'cape'.

This story, with a beginning that reminds one of *King Lear*, has been collected throughout Europe in more than two dozen different versions, and belongs to the very large group of tales (there are more than three hundred of them) known as Cinderella stories.